For example, when the black hen
laid three eggs in one day,
Gregorie Peck laid four.

When the magpie laid an egg
high up in the gutter,
Gregorie Peck laid one on the chimney.

Gregorie Peck

by Geraldine McCaughrean
Illustrated by Colin Smithson

Gregorie Peck is a fine hen.
But she does like to go one better.

When the duck laid a blue egg,
Gregorie laid one freckled
and speckled with every shade of brown.

Then one day, floating high above the farmyard, the animals saw an egg bigger than anything they had ever seen before. It was a bright, shiny red egg.

"Whoever could have laid it?" gasped
the duck.
"However big is the mother?" wondered
the goose.
"No ordinary bird," said the turkey.

Gregorie Peck fluffed up her feathers.
"Call that an egg?" she swaggered.
"I can do better than that!"

So she sat down and tried very hard.
She laid the biggest egg
she had ever laid in all her life.

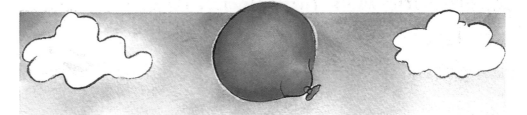

"But it isn't red," said the duck.
"And it isn't nearly as big," said the goose.
"And it doesn't fly through the air,"
said the turkey.

So Gregorie Peck flew up on to the farmhouse roof and tried as hard as she possibly could.

The animals down below were not very impressed.
"Come down immediately!" commanded the rooster.

The big red egg floated down to the ground.
It rolled under a cart and stayed there.
"Is it ready to hatch?" wondered the
animals.

"And what will hatch out?!"

"The mother is sure to come looking
for it," said the black hen.
"We should look after it until she comes.
Otherwise, she will be angry with us!"

The animals all agreed.
Somebody must sit on the egg
to keep it warm and safe.
But who would sit on the egg?

15

"I can't," said the black hen.
"I'm afraid of high places!"

"I can't," said the turkey.
"It might hatch out and eat me!

"I can't," said the duck. "I have eggs of my own to hatch."

"I can't," said Blue Moo the cow. "I would squash it for sure!"

Gregorie Peck
plucked up
all her courage:

pluck-pluck-pluck.

She marched over to the big red egg.
"I shall sit on the egg until it
hatches or until the mother comes."
It was her finest hour.

So Gregorie pulled out the
shining red egg
from under the cart,
and climbed on to its
squeaky red dome.

It wasn't easy,
but she did it.

But the egg did not hatch.
It floated upwards again
into the sky.

It floated higher than the gutter
where the magpie had laid its egg.
It floated higher than the chimney
where Gregorie had gone one better.
Gregorie began to slip.
So she dug in her claws.

Just then the sky was filled with roaring.
The other animals in the farmyard
hid their heads.
But looking up at the sky,
Gregorie Peck enjoyed her proudest
moment.
"Me! I did it! No one else!"

"I hatched out an aeroplane!"